CHARLIE AND THE MAGIC SPACESHIP

A Children's Book about Confidence, Respect and Inner-Strength | Present for Girls and Boys

RONALD WALLIAMS

THIS BOOK BELONGS TO

....

....

CONTENTS

CHARLIE AND THE SPACE RANGERS

Charlie was a kind little boy who was always ready for his next adventure. One time, his mum and dad gave him a new set of space rangers and he couldn't believe his luck! He wanted to take them on adventures so much, but it was nearly time for bed.

Before Charlie turned out his light he lined them all up by his window and wished them good night. What happened next would change his life...

As Charlie fell fast asleep he soon started to feel different like never before. The space rangers were his new best friends and they were all appearing in his dreams. The only thing was his dreams were so real that he thought he must still be awake.

Before Charlie could figure out what was going on he was looking at the most incredible spaceship he had ever seen. It was a giant rocket that was in every colour he had seen, and even some brand-new colours no one else had told him about. This must be magic he thought. But why was he dreaming about this?

Rather than trying to wake up, Charlie decided to follow the space rangers and listen to what they were telling him. They each had a unique and special skill and they wanted to invite Charlie into the spaceship to tell him more. He couldn't believe how amazing this dream was.

He took the first step up the steps into the giant rocket and suddenly he was transported into a completely different world. He felt all his weight disappear and he flew the rest of the way right into the spaceship. This was the most amazing thing he had ever seen.

Inside he found buttons that were changing colour, appearing in all sorts of different shapes, and making amazing sounds all at the same time. The space rangers told him they would teach him all about how the magic spaceship worked. Now it was his to enjoy every night when he went to bed.

He soon realised he wasn't dreaming at all. What he was doing was experiencing magic for the very first time. The spaceship was real and only Charlie could see it thanks to his amazing new space ranger friends.

Charlie was amazed by everything he saw and wanted to start his next adventure right away. Before the spaceship could launch he needed to get his special space suit from the equipment room. It was the perfect size and popped right onto him without him even having to pick it up. This really was amazing magic!

As Charlie looked all around him he saw that the suit was really big and strong so that it would keep him safe, but it was also so light he didn't even feel it slowing him down. This was the wonder of magic and it was something he could enjoy every time at bedtime.

Soon, he was sat in his command chair in the spaceship and the whole room was rumbling. Bubbles were coming past the windows in every colour of the rainbow. They were what powered the spaceship and made the magic possible, the space rangers told him. Charlie was amazed and just wanted to take it all in.

As the spaceship stopped rumbling it started making a whistling sound. They were travelling back in time to see whatever Charlie wanted. Would it be dinosaurs? Would it be pirates? Or would it be right back to the Big Bang? Before they could do any of these amazing things, Charlie first had to learn how to fly the spaceship.

The weird thing was the spaceship seemed to fly itself. Every time Charlie looked at the controls they seemed to change. How on earth would he make it go left, right, up, down?

He asked the head space ranger and he told him that all he had to do was be kind to everyone he met. The spaceship's magic would only work if he was kind during the day. If he was rude or nasty to someone then the spaceship wouldn't fly, and it certainly wouldn't change its controls so that Charlie could go exactly where he'd always dreamed of going.

Charlie thought about it for a minute and started thinking how strange this was. Could being kind really control a magical spaceship? What if he wanted to take it during the day? And why had he been chosen to get this magical spaceship? He'd never heard of other little boys getting one!

Kindness was like a superpower. Sometimes you could use it to make someone new feel welcome. When someone is new everyone else is often a little bit naughty. Being kind to the new person is the bravest thing you can do.

Sometimes, there's someone you don't like but you need to help them. Being kind to them is the bravest thing you can do. To be a space ranger you have to be brave to go and explore mysterious new galaxies, and to be brave you have to be kind.

Everyone had always told Charlie and his parents what a kind and gentle little boy he was. The space rangers had chosen Charlie because of how kind he was, but he could only keep his spaceship if he stayed himself.

As soon as Charlie realised this, he knew he was going to enjoy many more adventures in his magical spaceship. After spending all night whizzing past stars and zooming past meteors the spaceship returned to earth. Charlie waved goodbye to the space rangers, saw the bubbles pop, and woke up in bed to the sound of his mum.

He had the biggest smile on his face and couldn't wait to tell her all about his amazing dream. His mum knew Charlie had some vivid dreams, so she had no idea that he'd experienced real magic.

This would be Charlie's little secret to enjoy for years, and he couldn't be happier.

CHARLIE AND THE POCKET-SIZED GALAXY

One night, Charlie was trying to get to sleep. He knew that the moment he fell asleep he would get to ride on his spaceship, but he couldn't quite seem to get comfortable. Something was bothering him.

No matter how tight he closed his eyes he kept seeing a blue light coming from somewhere in his room. He turned off his TV, he didn't have a phone, and none of his toys had lights. What on earth could it be? Soon, Charlie started to think there was something magical in the room...

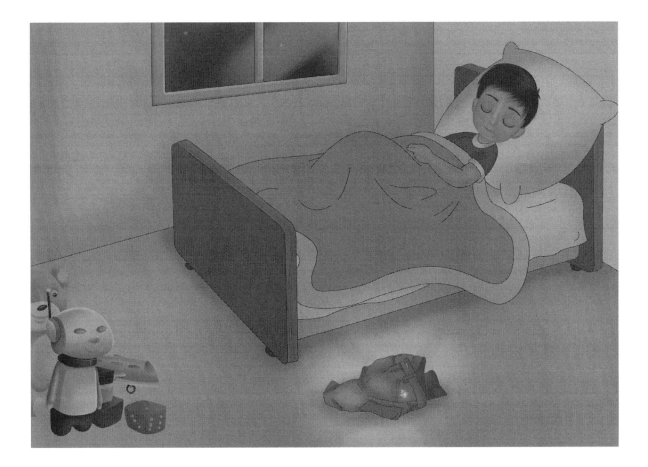

He wanted to get on the spaceship so badly that he did something he had never done before. He gave up on trying to sleep and started walking around his room, trying to find where the blue light was coming from. He realised that there was a funny popping sound coming from his trousers that were lying on the floor. There was a blue light flashing from inside them and he had no idea what it was. Could it be dangerous? Was it some extra magic?

Charlie picked up his trousers and turned out the pockets. Something landed on the floor, but it made no sound. As he looked down he saw it hovering gently above the ground. It must be magic because it was just floating there. That's why it didn't make a sound when it hit the ground!

He picked it up and felt a warm glow which was like a giant cuddle. The blue lights seemed to be coming from a little whizzing mini galaxy that was so realistic Charlie didn't know what to make of it. He'd seen similar toys in the toy store before, but none of them looked this realistic.

As Charlie was about to put it on his bedside table and try and go back to sleep he remembered something. He'd never even asked for this toy! How could it have possibly appeared in his trousers during bedtime? This must be magic he thought!

With no grown-ups around to ask, Charlie decided to look closer all by himself. The warm glow was amazing and it seemed to be making a gentle whispering sound. Charlie picked it up and put it closer to his ear. That's when he saw out of the corner of his eye his space rangers were moving towards him and asking him what he'd found. They were as amazed as he was.

One of them told him that he'd found his very own mini galaxy and that he had to be very careful with it. For the magic to last he had to make sure no one could ever find it, so how could he hide it? His mum and dad would easily see the blue light flashing away under his bedroom door so he had to think quick. When he asked the space rangers about how to hide it the answer amazed him.

They told him if he held it in his hand, laid down in bed, and counted to 10 then he would instantly be asleep and inside the magic spaceship.

He did exactly what they said and before he could finish saying the last number he saw bubbles out of the corner of his eye. He was back aboard the spaceship and the space rangers were right by his side again. It was amazing!

The space rangers told Charlie that the mini galaxy contained amazing things no one had ever heard of. They also told him that when you went inside, it was just as big as a real galaxy. The mini galaxy was a portal to another world, and it was Charlie's to look after.

The rangers took Charlie on an adventure so he could see just how amazing this new galaxy was. The stars were blue and green, the sky was red and yellow, and the water seemed to flow uphill, not downhill. Every planet seemed to have something completely different about it that no one on Earth would ever believe. This was a galaxy where everything was different and everything was amazing.

Why is it so different? He started thinking. Soon, one of the space rangers came and told him that this galaxy was actually his own galaxy but 1 million years in the future. Everything was different and everything had evolved. Charlie had been blessed with a magical gift, but why?

He was told that to make the magic last he had to keep this a secret and hide the mini galaxy from everyone. The space rangers from the future had sent it back in time to Charlie so that he could look after it because they knew how brave he was. They told him all about how they knew Charlie always helped new people at school. They also told him they knew if there was a fight at school and everyone was watching, Charlie was always the first one in the middle to break it up.

These were truly brave and courageous actions that the space rangers of the future loved about Charlie. He was the one person on Earth in the present time that they knew was brave enough to look after the mini galaxy. Everyone else on earth would want to show it off and try to brag, but they knew Charlie had so much kindness deep within his heart. He would do the right thing to make sure that the future was never destroyed and the space rangers could trust him.

As the magical spaceship got ready to land and the bubbles started to pop, Charlie's own space rangers told him the mini galaxy could stay on the spaceship. It would be safe there because Charlie was the only one who was brave enough for his dreams to take him aboard.

Suddenly, there was a loud pop as the final bubble burst and Charlie's mum walked into the room. The sunshine was coming in through the window and it was time for school. When she asked him what he dreamed about last night he had a quiet smile on his face and said nothing at all.

CHARLIE COMES UP WITH AN IDEA

Charlie was loving getting to explore things on his magical spaceship every night, but he knew he couldn't tell too many people about it. In fact, he'd been sworn to secrecy since it appeared that night.

The space rangers wanted to make sure the mini galaxy was protected, and they knew Charlie was brave enough to do it. But Charlie was different to every other little boy he knew because he always wanted to help people.

Charlie didn't care about doing things just to be popular, just like he didn't want to only help his friends. In fact, Charlie would help anyone because he knew it was the right thing to do. What made Charlie's way of helping people truly great was that he didn't do it just to be popular. He did it because he knew it was the right thing to do. That's when Charlie came up with an idea that would change how he was using the magical spaceship.

He loved having adventures and seeing new and amazing things, but he also wanted to help people. This is what made him so brave and courageous because he always put others first. He wanted to use the magic to figure things out that would help people so he could make their lives better without having to break the secret of the magic.

Earlier that day in school, a new girl joined the class. She had freckles, red hair and different types of clothes to everyone else in the school. She was a little bit different because she came from a different part of the country, but the sad thing is the other kids made fun of her. They didn't like her because she was different, but they also didn't really know her. Charlie knew he could use the magic on the spaceship to help the girl.

As he drifted off to sleep and started hearing the popping of the bubbles he was already getting excited. The spaceship launched and he was chatting away to the space rangers about how he needed to help the girl.

They were all so surprised because they'd planned another adventure to show Charlie amazing things. How were they going to do what Charlie wanted while also taking him around the galaxy tonight?

Charlie told his rangers he didn't care about missing an adventure; all he wanted to do was help. The rangers saw this was a truly brave little boy because he was willing to put his own fun second so he could help someone else. He was doing it even though it was someone he didn't really know yet!

He landed the spaceship on a rocky asteroid so they could all concentrate on what Charlie had to say. He wanted to use all the amazing magic inside the spaceship to come up with an idea about how to help the girl, but what would that even look like?

They told him about a special kind of magic where you could jump one month into the future and then make a little change that would change the present. They said it was very dangerous because if you made the wrong change you'd be stuck in the future forever and you'd never get to come back. They thought this was enough to put Charlie off so they could go on the mission they planned, but Charlie had other ideas...

Before they could even stop him, Charlie was pressing the buttons and saying the magic words they had told him about. A giant bubble carried Charlie into the future in an instant and he was right back in school. Everything looked just like it had done before he went to sleep, so what was different?

He looked around the classroom and saw that the new girl was still there, sitting alone and looking really sad. Everyone was ignoring her and she had no friends at all. How could this be after one whole month?

At the front of the class the most popular and funny boy was giving a speech for the class contest. Everyone was laughing and that's what made him so popular. The problem is that the new girl was so scared and shy after one month with no new friends that she really didn't want to speak. She was next and had no idea what she was going to say. She looked like she was about to cry.

Charlie rubbed his hands together really fast as he sneaked around the classroom so no one could see him. Out popped a completely new speech!

As if by magic it appeared on the girl's page and she never even noticed. He sat there at the back of the class, invisible, and hoping his idea had worked.

One minute later the whole class was laughing louder than Charlie had ever heard. The amazing thing was they were not laughing at the end of the speech of the funny boy — they were laughing with the new girl.

No one had taken the time to get to know her, so Charlie had given her the funniest, most amazing speech anyone had ever heard. It told them all about her amazing adventures before she came to her new school and everyone thought she was hilarious.

As she went back to her seat she seemed to be the only one who could see Charlie and she was smiling at him. Charlie knew he was invisible, but he also knew it was a good sign that the person he helped could see him.

He said the magic words, rubbed his hands together really fast, and closed his eyes as tight as he could. Before he knew it the space rangers were serving him his favourite drink and the tastiest cake he had ever tasted.

They told him how brave he'd been to risk something important to him for someone he barely knew. It was what being a kind, brave, and courageous little boy was all about.
It was also a mission Charlie would never forget.

CHARLIE LEARNS FROM HIS MINI CLONE

Charlie's adventures were getting more and more amazing with every passing night.

The highlight of his day was drifting off to sleep and setting foot aboard the magic spaceship.

One night, Charlie started to think about what would happen if he met himself. He wondered if the magic would let him create a clone so he could learn more about who he was and do an even better job with helping other people. He asked the space rangers and they told him they could, but there would be one crucial difference.

Charlie could create a mini clone of himself, not a full-sized version. This was to make sure the space rangers could tell the difference and the correct Charlie would wake up in his bed in the morning. Charlie thought for a little minute, saw this made perfect sense, and decided he wanted to try it.

He asked a space ranger for the magic words and he began rubbing his hands together and saying them aloud. Before he knew it, he was stood back in his bedroom with his miniature clone. He was so small he looked more like an action figure, but he was talking and moving just like Charlie. He wanted to know how he could use the clone to learn more about himself and how he could help people.

The space rangers told him he could take the clone to a parallel universe where everyone was tiny and everything was tiny, so it looked exactly the same. The only difference is the real Charlie would be massive so he had to use some extra magic to go invisible and weigh nothing. Charlie repeated the magic words, saw the bubbles coming out of the back of the spaceship, and started on his way.

Charlie's clone was talking to him just like Charlie would talk to himself in his head. This was amazing he thought, so he listened to everything he had to say. They seemed to be good company, and after all, he was just hanging out with himself! He told the clone he wanted to follow him and not speak to anyone so he could learn more about how other people saw him. The clone thought this was interesting because he'd never heard of a little boy wanting to do this.

The clone led the way and the real Charlie was walking behind, completely invisible and silent so nobody knew he was there. They went into school together and the real Charlie watched as his clone said hello to everyone and made his way to his desk. But there was something he noticed that really surprised him...

There was a boy called Simon in his class who Charlie had known for a couple of years but never really played with outside school. He'd walked right past Simon today without looking at him and hadn't even realised it. Why did this matter? Because Simon had big red puffy eyes like he'd been crying at break time.

His friends were laughing and joking all around him, but Simon just didn't seem interested. This wasn't the Simon Charlie knew.

He walked silently over to his clone and whispered something in his ear. The clone knew exactly what Charlie was saying and apologised to Charlie for not seeing Simon. They rubbed their hands together and went back in time by one minute. Once again they were walking in through the classroom saying hello to everyone. Simon was sat in the corner, sad just like he had been the first time. This time both Charlies walked up to him and asked him if he was okay. Simon was stunned.

Nobody had asked him if he was okay that day, and he started to think that no one would. He had a really bad tummy ache because he'd eaten something bad the night before. He was too shy to tell the teacher and he didn't want to tell his friends because he thought they would laugh at him. Charlie saw straight away what he needed to do. He sent his clone over to talk to the teacher and whisper in her ear.

When everyone was distracted with some colouring, the teacher walked over to Simon without anyone noticing, except the two Charlies. She told him that if he needed to go home she could call his mum and everything would be okay. Simon's face lit up with happiness and he gave the two Charlies a sparkling wink. Somehow he knew the real Charlie was in the room too.

The real Charlie told his miniature clone it was time to go back to the spaceship. He rubbed his hands together and said the magic words under his breath and with one loud pop he was back aboard. He told the space rangers about the clone and how he'd used it. They were all amazed.

Charlie had used the clone to think carefully about the way he was treating people. Not just his best friends, but the people around him who sometimes needed him but didn't know how to ask. By thinking about how he would react in a certain situation, Charlie had found a way to be even more kind. And because he had done it the right way, Simon could sense the magic too. Thinking carefully about how you treat other people, and how you can make them feel happy, really is a form of magic, Charlie thought.

With that special thought whizzing around inside his head, he wished the space rangers well and heard one last big pop as the final bubble burst. The next thing he saw was his mum walking into the room with a big smile on her face.

She knew her brave little boy was always thinking about other people, and that was real magic.

CHARLIE AND THE FLYING SCIENCE LAB

Charlie had been thinking all day about how he could help people. He soon realised magic wasn't the only answer, but it was how you decided to use the magic that mattered. He was thinking how he could create something that could make his friend better.

His friend Alice always seemed to have a runny nose, but no one seemed to care. She was just snotty and a lot of the kids were used to it. While no one made fun of her about it, Charlie knew it had to be really uncomfortable. Her parents didn't seem to know what to do, and they didn't seem that concerned. But had anyone stopped to ask Alice?

When they were playing in the park before tea he asked her what having a runny nose all the time felt like. She said she was used to it and it was all she knew, but sometimes her skin would be sore. Other times, it would get a bit itchy, and it was always very messy. Charlie felt bad for her but didn't want to make her feel bad by saying he thought there was something wrong. Charlie kept his feelings to himself because he didn't want to scare his friend or make her feel different.

Instead of worrying her, or causing her parents more stress, Charlie decided to use his magic aboard the spaceship that night. He was going to find a solution no one else had thought of and give it to her for nothing. This is what being kind and brave is all about. Taking on other problems and helping people in a way that makes them feel good about themselves again. Charlie was exactly the kind of boy who was great at doing things like this.

Charlie was closing his eyes as tight as possible and drifting off to sleep as fast as possible. With a loud pop and a giant bubble, Charlie was aboard the magical spaceship once again. He asked the space rangers

what he could do to help and he was amazed
by what they told him. They said there was an
entire science lab inside the spaceship that
could be opened with kindness.

Why kindness? Because being kind
is like magic and it could open doors in
so many ways. It makes people like you, it
makes people want to help you, and most
importantly of all it makes people happier.
Charlie's hand touched the door handle and

the lab opened right before his eyes. What he saw inside was truly amazing.

There were potions whizzing around the room, there were microscopes everywhere, and there was also a floating runny nose. He'd never seen a nose float in the air, and he'd never seen a nose all by itself before. There was so much snot running out of the nose and he saw it looked exactly like Alice's nose. Why was it here? So he could help make Alice better!

He got to work with the space rangers and they showed him how to mix potions so they whizzed around the room even faster. Each one flew up the runny nose and tried to help. One by one, they each got sneezed out and carried on whizzing around the room, changing colour as they went. The magic was trying every possible combination of ingredients to find a cure.

After a couple of hours, a bottle full of magical little rainbows flew up the nose and the nose instantly stopped running. Charlie was delighted because he knew he'd found something that would make Alice happy. But how could he give them to her without breaking the spell of the magic?

The space rangers told Charlie that if they gave Charlie the potion, and Charlie gave it to Alice without asking for anything in return, then the magic would still work. But, if Charlie asked for a favour or to swap a toy for the potion, it would never be able to help Alice again!

Charlie knew being kind is not about asking for favours or trying to get money. He knew it was just about making people happy by helping them in any way you could. He didn't have to think twice about giving the potion to Alice and he never thought about asking for anything in return.

Charlie wanted to wake up and see his friends smiling in school, and that's exactly what happened. Alice was smiling so much you could tell she was happier than she'd been in ages. She was telling everyone about how well she was doing and everyone was congratulating her. Her body must've got really strong overnight and it was all because she was such a lovely little girl.

Instead of getting jealous that no one was thanking him, Charlie just stood in the background and smiled. He knew it was the magic that had solved Alice's runny nose, but he didn't care. He just wanted his friend to feel happier and for people to be proud of her, so he let it all happen.

When Alice came over and told Charlie all about her runny nose he had to pretend he knew nothing about it. He asked her how she'd done it and she told him it must be magic!

Charlie let out the biggest grin he'd ever had and no one was any the wiser.

THE DAY CHARLIE DISCOVERED THE INTERGALACTIC SNACKS

One day, Charlie had given all his snacks to his big sister. He wanted to do it because she'd been sad that she'd fallen out with one of her best friends. Charlie didn't think twice about giving her his sweets, but now he had to admit he was a little bit hungry!

Because of all the amazing things he had learnt with the space rangers, he knew that asking her for the sweets back wasn't a kind thing to do. It would make her feel bad and like she owed him something. That's the last thing she wanted to hear.

Charlie got ready for bed and decided he was going to ask the space rangers to help him find some tasty snacks. One day, he might even invite his sister aboard to share them, but first he had to discover them. He shut his eyes as tight as he could, counted to

10, and before long he heard a giant pop as the bubbles started.

He was back aboard the magical spaceship and telling the space rangers all about what he wanted to do. They thought it would be a great idea, especially because he'd been so kind to his sister. These kinds of missions would be great rewards for Charlie and help him continue to grow as he wanted to become the kindest and most caring boy in the whole world.

The most senior space ranger told him all about a magical planet that was made of candy floss. The only problem was you could never take the snacks back to Earth. This was because the magic would be broken and they would disappear if you tried to take them anywhere except for the planet or the spaceship. Charlie was excited to see what it would look like and really excited to find out what it would taste like. They rubbed their hands together and the spaceship did the rest.

Before long, the spaceship was touching down and landed on the big squishy planet. It seemed to sink into the candy floss and then gently bounce back. Charlie jumped out and felt the same squishy feeling underneath his little feet. This was amazing he thought.

The space raiders began to get all sorts of magic tools out of the spaceship and they started digging out the candy floss without anyone touching them. This was more magic and just went to show that when you do something to help other people, magic things will happen for you too.

Charlie sat and watched the tools as they put more and more candy floss into one tiny bucket. There seemed to be no end to how much candy floss they could fit into this tiny bucket.

Before Charlie could get nervous about how hard it would be to lift such a heavy little bucket, the bucket flew along by his hand and didn't weigh anything. It was more amazing magic and it wowed Charlie every time he saw it. What amazed him even more is the bucket started speaking and said that this was a gift, a magical gift that was just for Charlie to thank him for all the amazing things he'd done recently.

Somehow, the rest of the universe knew how kind Charlie had been, so they rewarded him with more than he could ever wish for. The most important thing is that Charlie had never asked for a never-ending bucket of candy floss, which is exactly why it was given to him.

Charlie realised that being kind isn't just about helping people in the moment, it's also about making them feel good about themselves. If you remind someone that they owe you a favour because you were kind to them, the magic disappears before your eyes. Charlie never did that, which is why the bucket was his.

The bucket floated up the steps into the spaceship and then kept whizzing out every flavour of candy floss that Charlie could ever imagine. One moment he tried peanut butter and jelly, then he had liquorice candy floss, washed down with cola candy floss. They were the most amazing flavours and you would never find them on Earth. He passed them around to all the space rangers.

When they started to eat their candy floss they smiled because they saw even more flavours were coming out of the bucket. It just went to show that the kinder you were, the more good things would happen to you. The only problem was that the bucket had to stay on the magical spaceship.

Charlie asked the space rangers why they thought this was, and they told him it was to stop other kids getting jealous. If the magic ever increased so Charlie could bring someone aboard, then of course he could share all the new flavours with them.

Before he knew it, Charlie had checked his magic watch and found that his mum was walking up the stairs, ready to wake him up. He had to rub his hands together and say the magic words to get back in bed with a flash, so he put down his bucket and got to work.

As mum walked in the door she saw Charlie was already awake, grinning from ear to ear. He couldn't have been happier and she could see that he was ready to go out into the world and be kind.

The best thing is that Charlie never told his mum about the magic bucket, and he definitely didn't brag to any of his friends at school. Being kind was like a superpower, but if you wanted the magic to stay, you had to be sincere too.

CHARLIE'S SECRET ALIEN DOG

With every space mission Charlie did he was finding new ways to be kind, brave, and courageous. He saw that he was helping people who needed it, and the world was becoming a better place because of it. That's why he decided to do something he'd never done before. He made a wish...

Suddenly, there was a crackling sound inside the spaceship and an alien dog appeared. He spoke perfect English and told Charlie all about the amazing things he could do. He was bright pink and had this incredible tail that never stopped moving, even when he was sat still. Charlie was amazed because he always wanted a pet and this one was exactly what he'd wished for.

The dog even told him that he could leave the spaceship and come home to stay with Charlie. He would go invisible so no one else could see him, and he would never bark so no one could hear him. He even had his own secret supply of alien doggy treats that he could eat without ever making a mess. It was the perfect dog Charlie had always wanted and he couldn't have been happier. But there was one small problem...

Charlie's new dog had never left the world of magic and come to the human world, so he felt a little bit scared. He knew sometimes Charlie would be out at school and that he wouldn't be able to come with him, and that made him sad. Charlie wanted the dog to come back with him so much that he knew he had to find a way to make him feel comfortable. He thought as hard as he could, closing his eyes and making a face. His brain was really working hard and he was getting hot. Then suddenly, he had the bright idea he'd been looking for!

Charlie would use his pocket money to get the dog things that he would love and that his parents would never get suspicious about. That way he could share his bedroom with the alien dog in a way that would make him happy. It also meant that the magic would never wear off because Charlie would be using the pocket money he'd worked hard for to help someone else. It didn't matter whether it was a magical dog or a real life human best friend that he was helping. As long as Charlie was being kind and generous by helping someone, the magic would keep working.

That first night when the dog came to sleep in the bedroom, Charlie decided to stay with him and miss out on the spaceship. It was the first time in weeks he'd not been aboard the spaceship, but he knew it was the right thing to do. As Charlie was about to fall asleep he suddenly noticed the dog was sniffing at the window.

Charlie tried to ignore the dog and hoped he would lie down to have a sleep, but the dog was getting anxious. Charlie knew he had to get up and look out the window, and when he did what he saw was amazing.

There was a giant green monster walking down the street roaring that it wanted to eat the dog. He'd never seen a monster like this, and the space rangers were millions of miles away aboard the spaceship.

The only magic Charlie could rely on right then was his own bravery, so he reached into himself and found it. There were no magic words to say and no magic bubbles that would appear. What Charlie had to do was look after his friend and be brave.

Before the dog knew what was going on, Charlie had hidden him under a blanket and opened the window. He let out the loudest roar the monster had ever heard and told him to go away. The monster didn't even think twice about roaring back and started running faster than he ever had. The monster was three times as big as Charlie, but was easily more than three times as scared. It showed Charlie just what you can do when you're brave, even when you're much smaller.

He heard some gentle clapping and looked under the blanket. The dog's paws were clapping together, cheering the hero that was Charlie. It was a great feeling to help his new best friend by scaring away that big green monster, and it made Charlie feel good too.

Charlie now knew he could scare off anything just by being brave. He didn't need to be bigger than the things he was scaring, and he didn't always have to have the magic of the space rangers by his side. All he needed was to be brave and focus on the person he was trying to help. It was the right thing to do, so it came naturally to a cute little boy like Charlie.

By now it had gotten really late and a storm had begun outside. Charlie always got nervous and scared during storms because he didn't like all the loud noises. Normally, he would go into bed with his mum and his dad, but he knew he couldn't leave the alien dog. The dog came from a world where this didn't even feel like a tiny storm because his planet was so much louder. He saw how brave Charlie was being by staying with him even though he wanted to leave, so the dog cuddled up to him and told Charlie everything would be okay.

It made Charlie smile to think the dog had recognised how he was feeling. They truly were the best of friends and they slept all night, giving each other the warmest, most comfortable cuddles either of them had ever had.

THE NIGHT CHARLIE'S ALIEN DOG ESCAPED

Charlie's alien dog had been his best friend for a few weeks now, so he knew that they were going to be best friends for life. They were kind to each other, they helped each other feel brave, and they were always there to give each other a cuddle at the end of another long adventure. The only problem was that one day, his dog escaped...

As Charlie was tossing and turning trying to get to sleep he suddenly heard a giant pop. It sounded like one of the giant bottles that ended Charlie's adventures, but he knew he was still wrapped up warm in bed at home. He didn't think much of it until a few minutes later. The leaves rustling outside in the wind normally made his alien dog a little scared and he normally would come to bed with him. When his intergalactic pooch was nowhere to be seen, Charlie knew exactly what had happened.

He closed his eyes tighter than they had ever been closed before and drifted off to sleep faster than he'd ever drifted off to sleep before. Before he knew it he was sat in the command chair of his magical spaceship, telling everyone about his missing alien dog. They knew where he'd gone, so Charlie listened to the advice and started to think about a plan.

The great thing about Charlie listening like this is that he was happy to hear ideas from people with more experience. This was the first time he'd had this problem and he knew he needed help. Charlie could've told everyone that he was going to be a hero and made them follow his ideas, but Charlie wasn't like that. He knew that when you listen to people they give you bright new ideas that burned as bright as a star in the night sky.

The space rangers told Charlie all about a giant asteroid that was covered in comfy dog kennels. Sometimes, alien dogs would wish they could go back there just to have a rest. This didn't mean they were unhappy or they were sad, it just meant they needed a little time to themselves and some rest.

The alien dog mustn't have known how to tell Charlie that he was getting a little bit tired from the constant adventures, so he tried to sneak off. Charlie felt sad that he hadn't realised his friend needed him a little more than he need his four-legged friend.

To help Charlie get there faster, the space rangers each repeated the magic words that would take them to the kennels. Bubbles appeared in every colour of the rainbow out of the back of the magical spaceship and they were soon on their way. Before he'd even finished one of the delicious snacks they had aboard, the spaceship was touching down and was surrounded by kennels.

Every single one of them looked the same, and there were more than he could count in a lifetime. He knew he had to be awake in a few hours before his mum came upstairs to get him ready for school. What would Charlie do?

Because Charlie was a clever and kind little boy he knew that it was the perfect time to listen to someone with more experience.

One of the space rangers had spent most of her life catching alien dogs to help their worried owners. Charlie asked her what he should do and she told him exactly what to do. It was so simple if you just asked for help at the right time.

The space ranger reached into her pocket and pulled out a magical looking whistle. Smoke and bubbles were coming out the ends and it was in more colours than Charlie could ever count. He'd never seen a whistle like this and yet there was something strangely familiar about it.

As he put it to his lips and blew he heard all of the funny names and silly games come to life that he used to play with his alien dog. The only difference was now they were so loud that they could be heard everywhere. This was amazing thought Charlie, and all he had to do was keep blowing it until his dog came back.

At first, he didn't hear anything, so the space rangers told him to stop blowing and start listening. Taking this little bit of advice from the space rangers was so important because Charlie started to hear paw steps in the distance. They were getting quicker and louder with every passing moment.

Just when Charlie was about to put the magical whistle to his lips and blow it again, his dog appeared from around the corner. He was delighted to see Charlie with his alien tail wagging in every direction all at once. Charlie told him he was sorry that he didn't realise he needed him, and the dog let him give him a big cuddle. They made a promise to listen to each other and to talk to each other even more so they always knew what the other one needed.

Once they were back aboard the magical spaceship, Charlie gave the alien dog his favourite snacks. You could see his ears wagging and his tail doing a little dance. It truly was the perfect end to a nerve jangling adventure. Once his dog was happy and well fed, Charlie rubbed his hands together and made a large bubblegum pop. In an instant he and his dog were transported back to his bedroom and were soon cuddling up on his bed.

Charlie was delighted that his friend had come home, but there was something he wanted to keep secret. He kept the magical whistle just in case his dog ran away again. He hid it under his pillow, closed his eyes, and went to sleep.

WHEN CHARLIE'S BIG SISTER CHASED AWAY THE MONSTER

Charlie had so much homework to do and he was so tired that he hadn't visited his magical spaceship for nearly a week. He didn't even feel sad because he was just so busy with his schoolwork that he hadn't even thought about it. The space rangers knew he was busy and he was tired, so they didn't put any pressure on him. Good friends like that always know how you're feeling and make sure they're always there for you when you need them.

As well as having the space rangers for best friends and an alien dog for adventures, Charlie also had a big sister who always looked out for him. She knew that Charlie was brave and full of courage, but she also knew he was still just a little boy. He could get scared just like everyone else, it's just that he pushed himself and thought of new ways to do things.

Because Charlie hadn't visited the magic spaceship and seen all the other galaxies for what felt like a long time, some of the naughty monsters from the other galaxies were trying to get his attention. They were greedy and very naughty because all they wanted was Charlie's attention. They didn't really care that Charlie had a lot of other things to do, and they just wanted him to stop everything and come play with them. When Charlie still hadn't visited they started to get angry with him.

That's why one day when Charlie was trying to play football in the park, heard a strange rustling from behind a tree. He hadn't heard anything like this unless he'd been on one of his adventures, so he started to wonder what it could be. He never thought that the naughty monsters would try to get to Earth and get his attention, especially when he was so busy and needed a rest.

Charlie carried on playing football with his big sister and didn't think anything more of it, but the rustling came back again. When he tried to score a goal he kicked the ball so far away that it rolled right behind this big tree. It was the same tree that the rustling had come from!

There was coughing and stomping and crying coming from behind the tree now. The noise was incredible and Charlie had no idea what was going on. Suddenly, his ball let out a loud hissing sound. Someone naughty had popped it and thrown it back at Charlie. He felt like he was going to cry, which is when his sister came out to help him.

She ran behind the tree and chased away whoever it was. She came back and told Charlie she thought it was a monster and was amazed to find Charlie smiling back at her. Shouldn't he be afraid? She asked him if he could explain the monster and he finally told her all about his magic spaceship. She was amazed but didn't quite believe him. He knew there was only one way to prove it to her...

As they popped themselves into the magic spaceship she couldn't quite believe it. Part of her was convinced Charlie was talking a complete load of rubbish. But then when the popping of the giant bubble started and she was greeted by the space rangers she knew Charlie was telling the truth. What a lovely little boy to have used all this in such a lovely way, and without making other people jealous.

Charlie was just as happy because he finally got to show his lovely big sister the amazing world he discovered many months ago. She was always there to try and help him and protect him because she was three years older.

It's what made them so close, and he hoped this would make them even closer. Making someone happy who would always help him was such a lovely thing for Charlie to do. What else would you expect from a boy like Charlie?

When his sister got aboard the spaceship she was greeted by all the space rangers. They brought her up-to-date with all of the amazing adventures that had been happening over the last few months, and she couldn't believe it. The amazing thing was she knew Charlie could've made her jealous and stopped her coming whenever they had one of their arguments. But she also knew that they would always make up because she was caring and Charlie was kind. It's the one thing that mum and dad loved about them more than anything else.

Charlie's sister Aimee was never sure of a question or two. In fact, she talked so much the space rangers had to take it in turns to tell her everything she wanted to know. They were getting so sleepy from answering so many of her questions, but they still loved having her with them. They knew how exciting it must be for her!

When Charlie told her that they had to be back in time so they were in bed before mum woke them up, she looked so sad. Aimee was worried that she might never get to come on the spaceship again because really it was just for Charlie. Charlie was never like that, and the last thing he wanted was for his sister to be jealous of him. He knew how lucky he was to have this amazing thing in his life, so he promised to share it with her.

He made her promise that she wouldn't make other children jealous at school about it by telling them everything, and she agreed without having to think twice.

They were both thinking exactly the same things which is what made them such a close brother and sister. With one last big pop they both woke up in their beds and skipped out their doors to give their mum a big hug. It was a lovely start to the day for mum, and it was one amazing adventure for Aimee.

It would be the first of so many more to come.

WHEN AIMEE MADE CHARLIE FEEL SAFE

Charlie's big sister Aimee had been coming on space missions with him for more than one week now. She loved every minute of it and kept a promise to never tell any of her friends. The last thing Charlie wanted to do was turn this spark of magic into something that would make other people jealous. Having something nice in your life is not a reason to tell everyone and make them jealous, he thought to himself. That's exactly why he and his sister used their adventures to do kind things and find out amazing things that would help other people.

They both started saying the magic words in bed at exactly the same time, giving a gentle knock on the wall between the rooms so they knew the perfect moment to say them. They both heard the same loud pop of the bubbles at the same time and wished the alien dog good night. He would stay cuddled up warm in Charlie's bed while they went and explored the universe.

Tonight, they would do something that they would remember for the rest of their lives. They were heading to this giant red planet they saw far away in the distance on many of their adventures but never made the time to go and visit. The space rangers had told them it was full of monsters made of fire, but they knew if they worked together they could explore it safely. They'd been excited about it all week, and tonight was the night they were going to finally visit it.

As they appeared in the spaceship and ate the delicious intergalactic snacks, they told the space rangers their plan.

One of them looked nervous, one of them looked tired, and two of them looked quite anxious. Charlie and Aimee told the space rangers they just couldn't do this mission without them. They reassured them, gave them a hug, and even shared some of the snacks. Even though there were already enough snacks to go round, their simple act of sharing brought everyone closer together

Charlie asked their advice so he could hear what they thought about the plan. One of them said that they were a bit nervous about how hot the fire would get, and Charlie listened. They talked together for a long time and decided that they should look at the magic for ice and water. It would keep them cool and make sure they could explore the planet nice and safely.

Everyone thought it was a good idea and everyone felt good about it. Just by listening to how they all felt, Charlie had brought the team closer together. He was proud and it showed him being brave wasn't always about being loud and fast. It was also about listening to how people felt.

The spaceship made its way to the red planet and because they had looked up the magic for ice and water, no one was hot inside. The spaceship was safe and they were nice and cool. They landed on the rocky planet and saw a giant volcano taller than anything on Earth. It was just amazing and it was everything Charlie and Aimee had ever dreamed of.

Then suddenly, they saw something that scared both of them. It was a giant red monster made of fire and they were feeling hot and sweaty the moment they saw him.

This monster was so big and scary he had found a way to beat their magic. He also found a way to imprison the space rangers on the spaceship. They were stuck inside in an instant and had no idea how it happened. Charlie and Aimee suddenly felt very alone. They had done so many adventures by now, but they had never done one without the fearless space rangers by their side. What were they going to do?

They decided that the only thing they could do was work together. Working together when you're both scared takes courage and bravery, which is exactly what these two children had. They knew each other so well that they knew their strengths and weaknesses. Aimee was older and bigger than Charlie so she took the lead and Charlie liked that about her. Charlie made it clear that he would support her and help her figure out what had gone wrong, because he was great with new ideas.

As they started to run up one of the volcanoes to get away from the monster they noticed he was following. He wasn't very fast, but he wasn't getting tired. They were getting tired because the volcano was so steep and the hill to the top was so long. The monster spent all of his time doing this, so he never really got tired. He was roaring and shouting like he was crazy, telling them he wanted to gobble them whole. Charlie and Aimee knew from the space rangers that if they got hurt or an accident happened on one of their adventures it would break the magic and they would be feeling exactly the same way in the real world.

They wouldn't just wake up and everything would be okay. Their mum would have to take them to the doctor and they might have to break the magic by telling her how it happened. They couldn't risk putting everything in danger and missing out their adventures like that, and that's before they even thought about the alien dog!

That's when Aimee realised what was wrong with the monster. He was angry and lonely and he was acting like a bully. She knew from school that bullies aren't always bad people. Sometimes they're just trying to get attention because they don't feel very happy inside. They do it by trying to upset and scare other people which is wrong, but they still need help.

She told Charlie if they both roared back at him and were really brave he'd realise there were some people he couldn't scare or bully.

They did the biggest roar they ever heard and the monster stopped in his tracks. He suddenly looked scared and looked like he might cry. Aimee and Charlie reached out, held his hands, and gave him a big hug. They told him he could come on their next adventure and that they would pick him up on the magical spaceship.

The monster told them they were the bravest and kindest little children he'd ever seen. He also told them he'd never had a real friend because he scared everyone away. The moment Aimee and Charlie told him they would be his friends he started smiling, got so much cooler, and gave them a big hug too.

It just goes to show you that being brave and being kind so often work together. You never know who needs help and how you can help them, unless you try.

DISCLAIMER

This book contains opinions and ideas of the author and is meant to teach the reader informative and helpful knowledge while due care should be taken by the user in the application of the information provided. The instructions and strategies are possibly not right for every reader and there is no guarantee that they work for everyone. Using this book and implementing the information/recipes therein contained is explicitly your own responsibility and risk. This work with all its contents, does not guarantee correctness, completion, quality or correctness of the provided information. Misinformation or misprints cannot be completely eliminated.